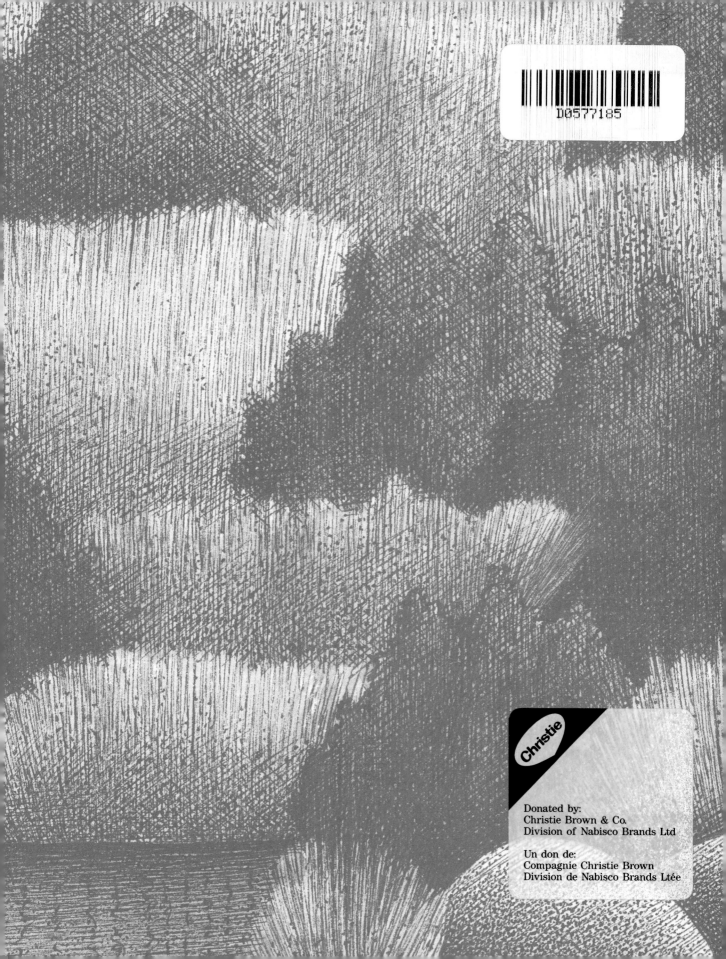

JADE AND IRON

Latin American Tales from Two Cultures

TRANSLATED BY
HUGH HAZELTON

EDITED BY
PATRICIA ALDANA

ILLUSTRATED BY
LUIS GARAY

A GROUNDWOOD BOOK

DOUGLAS & McINTYRE

TORONTO / VANCOUVER / BUFFALO

"The Legend of Manioc," retold by Joel Ruffino dos Santos, contemporary, from oral sources; "When Mountains Became Gods," retold by Carlos Franco Sodja in *Erase una vez en el Anáhuac* (1910); "Maichak," retold by the Ekaré Writers' Group, contemporary, from Gaylord Simpson in *Los indios de Kamarakoto* (1940) and Fray Cesareo de Armellada in *Tauron Panton* (1964); "Ñucu the Worm," retold by Jürgen Riester, contemporary, in *En busca de la Loma Santa*; "The Gods of Light," retold by Alicia Morel, contemporary, from oral sources; "How the Opossum Stole Fire," retold by Fernando Benítez, contemporary, from a story by Aurelio Kánare in *Los Indios de México*; Devil's Gorge, retold by Ana María Güiraldes, contemporary, from Oreste Plath in *Geografía del mito y la leyenda chilenas* (1970); "The Enchantress of Córdoba," retold by Francisco Serrano, contemporary, from texts by Luis González Obregón and Xavier Villaurrutia; "The Black Ship," retold by Pablo Antonio Cuadra in *Esos rostros que asoman en la multitud* (1930); "The Tears of Sombrero Grande," by Luis Alfredo Arango, contemporary, from oral sources; "Antonio and the Thief," retold by Saul Schkolnik, contemporary, from oral sources; "Pedro Rimales, the Healer," retold by Rafael Rivero Oramas, contemporary, from oral sources; "The Horse of Seven Colors," retold by Héctor Felipe Cruz Corzo, contemporary, from oral sources; "Blanca and the Wild Man," retold by Verónica Uribe and Carmen Diana Dearden, contemporary, from Santos Erminy Arismendi in *Huellas folklóricas*.

Translation copyright © 1996 by Hugh Hazelton
Illustrations copyright © 1996 by Luis Garay

Groundwood Books/Douglas & McIntyre Ltd.
585 Bloor Street West
Toronto, Ontario M6G 1K5

Distributed in the U.S. by Publishers Group West
4065 Hollis Street, Emeryville, CA 94608

The publisher gratefully acknowledges the assistance of the Canada Council and the Ontario Arts Council.

Library of Congress data is available

Canadian Cataloguing in Publication Data

Main entry under title:

Jade and iron : Latin American tales from two cultures

ISBN 0-88899-256-4

1. Tales - Latin America. 2. Indians of South America - Folklore. 3. Indians of Mexico - Folklore. I. Aldana, Patricia, 1946-   II. Garay, Luis, 1965-

PZ8.1.J33 1996   j398.2'098   C96-930393-9

Book design by Michael Solomon
The illustrations are done in pen and ink and watercolor
Printed and bound in Hong Kong
by Everbest Printing Co. Ltd.

CONTENTS

INTRODUCTION

WHAT we call Latin America stretches from Mexico to Argentina, from the Rio Grande in the north to the very tip of the South American continent, Tierra del Fuego. Many countries share this space. In some ways—climate, landscape, food, customs—they are very different from each other. But they also have things in common, perhaps the most important being language, Spanish and Portuguese.

All these countries were once inhabited by a rich variety of Native peoples. Although some lived in large, complex and very advanced empires, they were brutally conquered and then settled by Spanish and Portuguese warriors. Most of the original inhabitants died shortly after the arrival of the Europeans, through war, disease, or being worked to death. But some of the Native peoples have survived, although their lives are still frequently very difficult. Many of the original conquerors and those who came after them (now often called Latins) stayed. Some intermarried with Native people and created new cultures that were very different from those in Europe.

The tales in this book are drawn from a wealth of traditional stories, both Native and Latin, which have been passed down in oral and written form. They were first collected in a number of books that were published in many different Latin American countries. The Native stories, for the most part, explain in mythical form how the world and the things in the world that are important—food, fire, volcanoes—came to be. The Latin stories tend to be about people and their relationships with the natural world and each other.

Latin America is not a peaceful place. Many of the problems created at the time of the conquest have still not been resolved. Despite their tragic history, however, both Native and European Latin Americans have created a rich and complex culture. *Jade and Iron* (jade for the stone that was precious to the original inhabitants and iron, which was used by the Europeans for tools and weapons) is simply an introduction to the worlds that co-exist in Latin America and are still struggling to find a way to live together.

—Patricia Aldana

PART I

THE LEGEND OF MANIOC

BY **JOEL RUFFINO DOS SANTOS**

An Indian legend from southern Brazil

THERE was once an Indian girl named Atioló. In the season when the ground was covered with small yellow nance fruits, Atioló married Zatiamaré.

The nance fruits disappeared, and the waters of the river rose, flooding the soil. Then the sun burned the earth and a humid breeze came down from the mountains. When the nance began to fall like a yellow rain once again, Atioló was happy. She was pregnant and hoped to have a daughter.

Zatiamaré, though, felt differently.

"I want a son," he grumbled. "A son who will grow up to be just like his father. One who will hunt capybaras with a bow and arrow and paint his face with the bright red juice of annatto seeds, like me."

But the baby was a girl. Zatiamaré was so furious that he would not look at her face. He did not even give her a name. It was her mother who named her Mani.

The only present Zatiamaré gave his daughter was an iguana with a yellow tail. But he would not talk to her, oh, no. If Mani asked him something, he would answer with a hiss.

"Why don't you want to speak to your own daughter?" Atioló asked him sadly.

"Because she's not what I wanted," the father answered. "She's no more important to me than the wind."

Then Atioló became pregnant again.

"This time it had better be a boy who's just like his father," warned Zatiamaré. "If it's a girl I swear I'll abandon her in the treetops and won't even whistle to her."

And a boy was born, named Tarumá.

Zatiamaré did talk to him. He lifted Tarumá up on his shoulders when he crossed the river, and sat him on his lap to tell him stories.

Mani asked her mother to bury her alive. That way her father would be happy, and maybe she would be good for something. Atioló cried for days when she heard Mani's request. But her daughter pleaded so hard that in the end she agreed.

Atioló dug a shallow hole in the top of the hill behind their house and buried her daughter.

"If I need anything," Mani told her, "you'll know."

That night Atioló dreamed that her daughter felt very hot. Early the next morning she went back to the hilltop and dug her up again.

"Where do you want to be buried now?" she asked the girl.

"Someplace where there's more water," replied Mani. "Take me to the riverbank. If I don't feel right there, you'll know."

That night, Atioló did not dream about anything. She thought her daughter was happy in her new grave. The next afternoon, however, as she was bathing in the river, Mani's voice came floating over the water to her.

"Take me away from the riverbank. It's too cold to sleep here."

Atioló did as she asked. She took her daughter far away, deep into the forest.

"When you think of me," said the girl, "but can no longer remember my face, it will be time to visit me. Come back then."

Time passed. A great deal of time. One day Atioló thought of how much she missed her daughter, but she could not remember her face. She went into the forest, and on the girl's grave, she found a tall green plant.

"A plant this high couldn't be my daughter," she murmured.

At that very moment the plant divided in two. One part dragged itself slowly over the soil and turned into a root. Atioló decided to take this root home with her.

It was manioc, which would become the staple food for all the people.

WHEN MOUNTAINS BECAME GODS

BY **CARLOS FRANCO SODJA**

An Aztec legend from ancient Mexico

THE ARMY of the Aztec Empire was returning from war, but no one beat upon the *teponaxtle* drums, or blew into the sacred conch shells, or made the great *huehuetl* kettledrums reverberate through the streets and temples. Nor did the flutes spread their piercing notes over the vast valley of Anáhuac that the Aztecs called home. The shimmering blue-green waters of the five lakes—Chalco, Xochimilco, Texcoco, Ecatepec and Tzompanco—reflected the image of a miserable army that was returning in defeat. Eagle Knight, Jaguar Knight and Coyote Captain were all coming home with shattered shields, fallen plumes and ragged, bloody clothes that fluttered in the breeze.

The hearths were cold in the temples and fortresses as the men retreated, and the great earthen incense burners that bore the grim portrait of Texcatlipoca, the crippled god of war, were empty of the aromatic smoke of the *tlecáxitl* plant. The banners of the army were lowered in shame, and the council of elders, who were masters in the art of military strategy, anxiously awaited the warriors' arrival so they could hear the reasons for the defeat from the mouths of the soldiers themselves.

Much time had passed since a large and well-armed expedition had set out to conquer the Olmecs, Xicalancas, Zapotecs and Vixtotis who lived to the south, in order to expand still further the vast Aztec domain. Two lunar months had gone by. Many at home thought that a new colony had already been established, and yet now they found the crestfallen warriors sadly winding their way home.

During those two moons the soldiers had fought bravely, neither giving nor asking for quarter, yet in spite of their valor and the training they had received in the Calmecac, or academy of war, they now returned decimated,

their maces and war clubs cracked and dented, their shields battered and stained with enemy blood.

At the vanguard of this sad and disillusioned host strode an Aztec warrior who, despite his torn clothing and fallen crest of many-colored feathers, nevertheless retained an air of gallantry, haughtiness and pride.

The men of the country hid their faces, and the women wept and locked their children indoors so they would not witness such a dishonorable return. There was only one woman who did not cry. She stared in amazement at the Aztec warrior. His proud countenance and serene gaze showed how hard he had fought, though at last he and his men had been overcome in a valiant struggle against overwhelming numbers of enemy troops.

The watching woman turned as pale as the white lilies of the lakes as the warrior strode by, and his keen dark eyes suddenly locked onto hers. She was Xochiquetzal. Her name meant "Beautiful Flower," though now she felt that she was suddenly wilting, for this Aztec warrior was the man to whom she had once sworn eternal love.

Xochiquetzal looked away furiously. Only a week before, she had been married to a man from Tlaxcala. He had told her that the Aztec warrior, her true love, had fallen in the Zapotec War.

Now she turned to her new husband.

"You lied to me, you wretch! You're as hateful and venomous as a scorpion! You tricked me into marrying you. I don't love you and never will. He's the one I love, and always will love, too, now that he's come back."

Xochiquetzal threw insult after insult at her sly Tlaxcalan husband. Then, lifting up the hem of her long *huipilli* tunic, she ran off along the lakeshore, sobbing and lamenting her loss.

Her graceful silhouette was reflected in the iridescent surface of the waters of Lake Texcoco as she fled. The Aztec warrior turned again to look at her and saw that she was now being pursued by her husband and was obviously terrified. He clenched his hand on the hilt of his war club and, stepping out from the ranks of downcast soldiers, he ran after them.

The despicable husband had almost caught up to the beautiful Xochiquetzal when the Aztec warrior reached them both.

Neither man spoke, for the time for words and reason was past. The Tlaxcalan drew the short lance he carried beneath his cape, and the Aztec brandished his war club inset with the teeth of jaguars and wild boars.

Love and lies met in combat.

The lance with the barbed flint tip sought out the warrior's flesh, while the Aztec struck furiously at the Tlaxcalan with his serrated club, aiming his blows directly at the skull of the man who had stolen his beloved.

And thus they fought on, moving farther away from the valley, carrying their bitter battle into the lagoons, where transparent salamanders and bright green frogs skittered away from them over the slimy soil.

The battle continued for a long time.

The Tlaxcalan defended his wife and his lies. The Aztec fought for the woman he loved, whose image had given him the courage to return alive to Anáhuac.

Finally, when darkness was falling, the Aztec landed a mortal blow upon the Tlaxcalan, who turned and staggered away in the direction of his homeland, as if in search of help from his distant countrymen.

The victor, who had triumphed in the name of love and truth, now searched for his beloved Xochiquetzal.

He found her lying dead in the valley. She had not been able to live with the sorrow and shame of having been the bride of another man when she still loved the warrior to whom she had pledged her soul.

The Aztec knelt at her side and wept with his eyes and soul. He cut marigolds and flowers of bright yellow broom and covered the beautiful Xochiquetzal's still form. He crowned her temples with fragrant pink blossoms of *yoloxochitl*, the flower of the heart, and brought an incense burner and copal, a tree resin, while the Morning Star, the messenger of death, crossed the sky.

At that moment the earth suddenly trembled. A deafening thunderbolt struck out of the sky and an earthquake occurred that had never been prophesied by the wise men and soothsayers, nor predicted in the wondrous manuscripts of the priests. The land opened up and the sky darkened and fragments of fire fell into the five lakes, and the hearts of the people of Anáhuac were filled with fear.

At dawn two snow-covered mountains were standing where the valley had once been. One had the unmistakable form of a woman reclining on a mound of white flowers. The higher mountain had the shape of an Aztec warrior kneeling over a flowing mass of snowy hair.

The highland flowers that grew among the pines and morning dew covered the slopes of the dead woman's shape with a white shroud. The lovely white of dawn and freshly fallen snow lay on the breasts of the woman's form and spread across the rest of her body.

Ever since then, those two volcanoes have kept watch over the beautiful valley of Anáhuac. Their names are *Ixtacihuatl*, which means "Sleeping Woman," and *Popocateptl*, which is called "Smoking Mountain" because of the vapor that sometimes rises from its immense volcanic incense burner. The mountains received offerings of flowers and songs because of the water that ran down their slopes to irrigate and fertilize the fields of Anáhuac. And for many years, until just before the Conquest, young women who died unhappy in love were buried on the slopes of Ixtacihuatl.

As for the cowardly and deceitful Tlaxcalan husband, he became lost and died near his own land. He was also transformed into a snow-capped mountain called *Poyautecatl*, which means "Lord of the Dusk," and which was later known as *Citlaltepetl*, or "Mountain of the Star." It watches from afar over the eternal sleep of the two lovers whom it was never able to part.

MAICHAK

BY **THE EKARÉ WRITERS' GROUP**

A legend of the Pemon tribe of the plains of southern Venezuela

LONG ago, when people lived for hundreds of years, a man named Maichak had a hut on the slopes of Mount Auyan-tepuy. Maichak didn't know how to hunt or fish, or weave baskets, or make sieves for sifting manioc flour. He would go fishing without hooks or nets, and hunting without his bow and arrows. He always came back empty-handed, and his brothers-in-law laughed at him.

One day, when he had gone out fishing and not caught anything, as usual, he sat down sadly on the riverbank. Suddenly a little man popped out of the water in front of him.

"What's wrong, Maichak? Why can't you catch any fish?" he asked.

"I can't catch any because I don't know how to do anything," Maichak replied.

"Don't worry," said the little man. "I'm going to give you a cooking pot made from a *tapara* gourd."

"A cooking pot? What will I do with that?" asked Maichak.

"Whenever you put water from the river in the pot, the river will dry up and you'll be able to gather all the fish you want. But be careful. Only fill the pot halfway. If you fill it up completely, the water will spill over and flood the shore. And don't show it to anybody, or you'll lose it."

Maichak did as the little man in the river had said and finally was able to catch lots and lots of fish.

When he went back to the village, his brothers-in-law asked each other, "How was that numbskull able to catch so many fish?"

The days passed. Everyone wanted to know the secret of Maichak's success. But he said nothing.

One day, when Maichak was working in the family garden, his brothers-in-law looked through his shoulder bag and found the cooking pot. They took it down to the river to get a drink of water. When they filled it, they were shocked to see the river suddenly dry up.

"So that's how Maichak catches all those fish!" they said. "Now we know his secret."

They filled the pot again, but not knowing how to use it, they filled it up to the brim. The river immediately overflowed its banks and flooded the shore. The current washed away the little pot, and a huge fish rose out of the water and swallowed it.

Maichak became very sad. He searched for the little pot for months and months, but couldn't find it. Without it, he couldn't catch a single fish. He went out hunting and fishing as before, but always returned empty-handed.

One day, while he was hunting, he met an armadillo that was carrying a maraca rattle in its paw and singing a song that went, *I'm playing the maraca of the wild peccary pig. That's what I play! That's what I play!*

The armadillo repeated the song three times. Then it stood up on its hind legs, shook the maraca three more times, and dove into its burrow. A whole herd of peccaries immediately appeared, but since Maichak didn't have anything to hunt them with, he had to return home empty-handed once again.

Maichak decided to take the armadillo's maraca and use it to hunt peccaries, so he went back into the forest in search of the animal's burrow. The armadillo stuck its head out of the ground and sang its song, but when it reached over with its paw to shake the maraca, Maichak jumped up and grabbed the rattle away. He began to shake it, but the peccaries didn't come. The armadillo climbed out of its hole to see who had taken its maraca.

"Why did you take away my maraca?" it asked.

"Because I need it," answered Maichak. "I want to hunt peccaries."

"That's fine," replied the armadillo. "It's yours. But let me give you some advice. You had a cooking pot made from a *táparo* gourd, and you lost it. Don't lose the maraca. If you play it more than three times in a row, the peccaries will come and take it away from you."

From that day on, Maichak always came home with lots of fresh peccary meat. His brothers-in-law were amazed and began to keep an eye on him.

One day, when Maichak went out hunting, one of his brothers-in-law followed him to see how he was able to bring back so many peccaries. The brother-in-law heard him singing and playing the maraca. He hid in the underbrush and saw where Maichak concealed the instrument.

When Maichak returned home, the brother-in-law took the maraca and sang the same song he had heard Maichak singing. Then he shook the maraca four or five times.

Suddenly an enormous herd of peccaries appeared, surrounded the brother-in-law and took away the maraca.

When Maichak went back to the forest to look for his maraca, he realized it was gone. He had lost it, just as he had lost the cooking pot.

He spent days and days searching for the maraca. One afternoon, when he was tired of looking, he came upon a howler monkey that was combing its mane of fur. Large numbers of birds flew up and landed near the monkey as it preened itself.

"Let me have the comb there, brother," said Maichak.

"I can't," the monkey replied. "It's the only one I have."

But Maichak kept pleading until the monkey finally gave the comb to him. As he did so, he said, "All right then, it's yours. But don't comb yourself more than three times in a row, because the birds will come and take it from you."

"That's all right," said Maichak. "I understand."

From then on, Maichak always came home with lots of delicious birds for dinner. And, just as before, his brothers-in-law started to spy on him.

When they saw what Maichak did with the comb, they waited until he left to go and work in the fields. Then they searched his bag. When they found the comb, they went out to hunt birds.

But they didn't know the comb's secret and ran it through their hair so hard that whole clouds of birds, including wild turkeys and curassows, began to circle overhead and then snatched the comb away.

When Maichak came home from the fields and saw that his comb had disappeared, he became very sad. Then he grew angry with his brothers-in-law.

"Why do you always have to take everything away and lose it?" he asked. "You're a bunch of fools. Just keep on living right here, because I don't want to stay with you anymore. I'm leaving."

Maichak went far away and had wonderful adventures. He traveled to the world above, far beyond the clouds. He learned to hunt, fish and make sieves for sifting manioc.

Many moons later, he finally returned to his village. He told his family about the places he had visited and taught them all the things he had learned.

ÑUCU THE WORM

BY **JÜRGEN RIESTER**

A story of the Chimane Indians of the Bolivian Amazon

LONG, long ago, the sky was so close to the earth that sometimes it would crash into it, killing many people.

In one of the Chimane villages there lived a woman who was poor and alone. She often went hungry because she had no one to help her in the fields or find food.

One day, as she worked in her garden, she saw something shiny among the yucca plants. I wonder what it is? thought the woman, but she went home without looking further. That night she dreamed that the shining thing was moving, as if it were alive. In the morning she found it and wrapped it in a yucca leaf. She called it Ñucu and took it home and put it in a jug to feed it. From that time on she treated it as if it were her own child.

Ñucu looked like a white worm. By the end of the week he had grown so much that he filled up the entire jug. The woman had to make a larger vessel for the worm, but a week later, Ñucu had filled up that pot, too.

The poor woman was now working as hard as she could just to provide enough food for Ñucu, who was always extremely hungry.

After three weeks, Ñucu told her, "Mother, I'm going fishing."

That night he went down to the river and lay across it. His enormous body dammed up all the water, and the fish began to jump out onto the bank. At dawn the woman came and gathered up all the fish and put them in a basket. From that time on she always had enough to eat. Every night she would go down to the river with her son and run along the shore picking up fish and putting them in her basket.

People began to whisper, "Why does that old lady have so many fish these days, when before she was practically starving to death?"

They went to her and asked, "How did you get all the fish?"

The woman did not answer.

Time passed, and the people of the village began to have trouble finding enough to eat. There were not enough fish to go around, because Ñucu was catching them all.

So one day Ñucu said, "Mother, go ahead and tell them to come here and fish."

The woman went to the people of the village and said, "Ñucu is fishing upstream from here. Come on. He's invited us all to gather fish for everybody."

That was how the villagers discovered the old woman's secret. After that, things went well for everyone for a long time. Finally, though, Ñucu had grown so much that he could not fit in the river anymore. This time he told the old woman, "Mother, it's time for me to move on. You won't go hungry now, because the other villagers will know how to give you a hand. I've got to hold up the sky so that it won't ever fall in on the earth again."

Ñucu lay down across the earth from one end of the world to the other and lifted his body to hold up the sky, just as he is still doing today. As she looked up at the blue sky so far away, the old woman began to cry. But at night she could watch Ñucu shining high above. He was the Milky Way, and it comforted her to think that every night she would be able to see her son.

THE GODS OF LIGHT

BY **ALICIA MOREL**

A legend of the Mapuche Indians of central Chile

BEFORE the Mapuche people discovered how to make fire, they lived in caves in the mountains. Stone houses, they called them.

Ever fearful of volcanic eruptions and earthquakes, they worshiped gods and demons that were filled with light. Among them was the powerful deity known as Cheruve. When he became angry, great rocks and rivers of lava would rain down upon the earth. Sometimes Cheruve would fall from the sky in the form of a meteorite.

The Mapuches believed that their ancestors lived on in the arching vault of the night sky. Every star was a luminous forebear hunting ostriches among the galaxies.

The sun and moon were beneficent gods who gave life to the earth. The Mapuches called them Father and Mother. Each time the sun rose, they would greet it. The moon, which reappeared every twenty-eight days, divided time into months.

Since they did not yet know how to make fire, they ate their food raw. When it was cold at night they huddled together with their animals, including the dogs and llamas they had domesticated.

They had a horror of the dark. For them it was full of ghosts, demons and sorcerers. The song of the *chuncho* owl, in the night, was a sign of sickness and death.

They imagined terrible things.

In one of the Mapuche caves lived a family: Caleu, the father; Mallén, the mother; and Licán, their young daughter.

One night when Caleu raised his eyes to the sky to see his ancestors, he saw a strange new sign in the east—an enormous star with a golden tail. The bright celestial light was like that of the volcanoes. Would it bring misfortune?

Would it burn up the forests?

Worried as to what the star might mean, Caleu did not mention it to his wife or to the others who lived in caves nearby. But the other Indians soon also saw the fiery star in the night sky. They held meetings to discuss what this new sign might mean, and they decided to take turns observing it from the mouths of their caves.

Summer was drawing to a close. Early one morning, the women of the band climbed the slope of the mountain to gather wild plants that would provide them with food during the cold winter months ahead.

Mallén and her daughter Licán climbed the mountainside along with the other women.

"We'll bring back golden pine-nuts and dark red hazelnuts," Mallén told her husband.

"We'll bring back roots and cucumber-fruits from the *copihue* tree," Licán added. The girl had accompanied her mother on these excursions before and was in good spirits.

"Be back before nightfall," Caleu warned them.

"If it starts getting dark, we'll take refuge in one of the caves up there in the forest," replied Mallén.

The women carried baskets woven from the stems of climbing plants. They looked like a procession of *choroye* parrots, talking and laughing as they went up the mountainside.

On the slope above there were gigantic araucaria trees that rained down showers of pine-nuts. And the small round hazelnuts they found on the ground were shiny red, purple or black, depending on how ripe they were.

The women were not aware of how quickly time went by. Suddenly the sun began to set behind the mountains, and before they knew it, night was coming on.

Frightened, they put their baskets on their backs and took their children by the hand.

"Let's start back down!" they called out to each other.

"We don't have time. It's getting dark and we'll get lost in the night," warned Mallén.

"What shall we do, then?" asked Grandmother Collalla, who was the oldest of the women, though not necessarily the bravest.

"I know where there's a cave nearby," said Mallén. "Don't be afraid."

Mallén guided the women and their children along a rocky trail. It was nightfall by the time they reached the cave. In the eastern sky, they saw the huge star trailing its golden tail.

Grandmother Collalla became very afraid.

"That star is bringing a message from our ancestors who live in the dome of the sky," she exclaimed.

Licán and the other children clutched their mothers' skirts.

"Come on, everyone. Let's go into the cave and sleep all curled up together so we won't feel afraid," said Mallén.

"That's a good idea," answered the elderly Collalla, trembling with fear and cold.

Collalla knew the old stories. She had seen volcanoes explode, mountains collapse, floods cover the valleys, and forest fires rage through the woods.

As soon as they entered the cave, a deep noise from underground made them throw their arms around each other and pray to the sun and moon, their guardian spirits.

Then a terrifying earthquake caused bits of rock to fall from the roof of the cave. The women and children huddled together, terrified, in a corner.

Even when the earthquake was over, the mountain kept on shaking like the body of a frightened animal.

The women touched their children to see if anybody had been hurt, but everyone was all right. They breathed a bit easier and looked out of the mouth of the cave. Showers of small stones were falling down the slope above them, giving off sparks as they struck the rocks below.

"Look!" cried Collalla. "Stones of light! They're a gift from our ancestors!"

Like myriads of fireflies, the stones rolled down the mountainside, and their sparks set fire to a tall dry *coihue* tree that grew in the bottom of a ravine below.

The fire from the burning tree lit up the night, and the women and children calmed down when they saw its light.

"The star with the guardian spirit sent this fire so we wouldn't be afraid," laughed Grandmother Collalla.

The women and children also laughed and applauded the fire.

Then the group silently watched the flames as if the Sun Father himself had come down to be with them.

They sat together at the mouth of the cave, listening to the flames crackle like some unknown music.

A short time later, the men arrived, braving the darkness in search of their children and wives.

Caleu stepped close to the fire and picked up a burning branch. The other men did the same, and soon a flickering procession was making its way home down the mountainside.

The men set fire to other trees and bushes as guideposts as they went down the slope.

The next day, when the other Indians heard the story of the stones that gave off sparks, they went up the mountainside to collect them. They found that by striking them together next to dry leaves, they were able to light fires whenever they wanted.

They had discovered the stone known as flint. They had learned how to make fire.

Ever since that time, the Mapuches have had fire to give them light at night, to keep them warm, and to cook their food.

HOW THE OPOSSUM STOLE FIRE

BY **FERNANDO BENÍTEZ**

A legend of the Cora Indians of western Mexico

L ONG ago, people did not know what fire was. They lived on the roots of plants, sagebrush seeds and animal meat, all of which they ate raw. They had to eat everything without cooking it.

Our ancestors, the Great Ones as they are called in the Tabaosimoa language, met together and discussed how they could go about finding something that could warm them and with which they could cook their food. They debated it day and night. They even fasted and slept apart from their wives. Every day they saw the great fire that came out of the east, passed over their heads and then went down into the sea, but they were never able to touch it.

The Great Ones grew tired and finally called together all the peoples and animals of the earth.

"Brothers," they told them, "would any of you be able to bring us the fire that passes overhead every day?"

"Well," said one of the men, "five of us could go to the east where the sun rises and steal one of its rays, just one shaft of light from the fire in the sky that warms us every day."

"That sounds like a good idea," replied the Great Ones. "So it shall be. Let five men go to the east. We will stay here fasting and praying. Perhaps they will succeed in wresting a ray of light away from the sun, and we'll finally have what we've needed for so long."

Five men immediately set out and at last came to the hill from which the fire arose. They waited there for dawn. But when daylight came, they realized that the sun actually rose behind a second hill beyond the first one, so they continued their journey to the east.

When they arrived at the second hill, they saw that the sun seemed to come up behind a third hill that was much farther away. And thus they continued on, to a fourth and finally a fifth hill before they became discouraged and returned to the others, sad and tired.

"O Great Ones," they said. "We have traveled from hilltop to hilltop in pursuit of the sun, and we know now that we will never be able to catch up to it. This is why we're so sad. Sad and defeated."

"That's all right. You've carried out what you offered to do. Now you may rest. We will continue to think of how we might go about reaching the sun. We beg you with all our hearts to help us with your prayers and wise counsel."

Then Yaushu, the wise opossum, stepped forward. "Listen to me, O Great Ones! Once I traveled to the east and saw a light far away. I asked myself, 'What is that shining so brightly over there, at the farthest edge of my sight? I have to find out.'

"So I traveled toward it day and night. I gave up sleeping and almost gave up eating. I no longer thought about weariness. At the end of the fifth day, I saw a circle of logs burning at the entrance to an enormous cave. Flames from the fire leaped high into the air and gave off whirlwinds of sparks. An old man sat on a small bench, watching the circle of fire. He was tall and wore no clothes other than a loincloth of jaguar skin. His hair stood on end and his eyes gleamed fearfully. From time to time he would get up and throw branches and logs onto the blaze. I was afraid and hid behind a tree without daring to get any closer. Then, ever so slowly, I crept away. As I moved farther off from the circle of light, the heat grew less intense. 'It's something hot,' I said to myself. 'Something terrible and dangerous.' That was what I saw in the east, lords and fathers."

"And would you, Yaushu, be willing to return to that cave and bring us back a ray of that wonderful light?" asked the Great Ones.

"Yes, I am willing to go back there. But before I do, brothers and sisters, I ask you to fast for five days and pray to the gods for help and give them offerings of corn flour and cotton."

"We will do as you ask," said the Great Ones. "But you must know, Yaushu, that if you deceive us, we will kill you."

Yaushu smiled at them and said nothing. The Great Ones fasted for five days. As they did so they continuously begged the gods to grant Yaushu what he had desired for so many long years. When their fast was over, they gave

Yaushu five bags of corn flour with sage seeds.

"I'll be back soon," the opossum told them. "If all goes well, it should take about five days. Wait for me until after midnight. Put sleep aside and stay wide awake. There's a chance I might die. If that happens, please don't mourn or think back on me."

After saying this, Yaushu set off with the five bags of corn flour on his back. Five days later he found the same old man he had once seen, sitting on his bench and looking into the fire.

"Good evening, Grandfather," said Yaushu.

The old man did not answer.

"Good evening, Grandfather," Yaushu said again.

"What are you doing running around at this hour?" the Lord of Fire asked him.

"The elders, the Great Ones that live down below, have asked me to bring them some holy water."

"Why didn't you come earlier? This isn't the right time," said the old man.

"I'm the Great Ones' messenger," replied Yaushu. "I'm very tired, and all I ask is that you let me sleep a bit here. By dawn tomorrow, I'll be on my way."

After pleading with the old man in his high little voice and using all his powers of persuasion, Yaushu finally convinced the Lord of Fire to let him bed down just outside the cave.

"All right. You can spend the night here, but don't touch anything," the old man warned him.

Yaushu sat down near the fire. He mixed some corn flour with water from the gourd he carried, dished it out onto two plates, and offered one of them to the Lord of Fire.

"If you're hungry, let me invite you to eat with me, even though my provisions are getting low and I still have a long way to go."

The old man smelled the corn flour, and the aroma went straight to his heart. He took the plate Yaushu offered him and poured a bit of the corn flour into the middle of the fire. Then he put his finger into the flour and water on his plate and picked up a bit of the paste. He threw a few drops of it over his shoulder and a few more on the ground. Then he began to eat. When he had finished, he gave the plate back to Yaushu.

"That corn meal of yours is quite tasty," he said. "It fills you right up, too.

May God bless you for sharing it with me. *She timua, tamashiten.*"

Yaushu stretched out his blanket a short distance from the cave. He was trying to think of some way he could steal a bit of the fire. After a while, he began to snore. Then the old man laid out a dried animal skin and rested his head on a rock. A short time later he got up, bowed to the fire and stirred up the flames. Then he lay down to rest again. The animal skin beneath him creaked for a few moments as he settled himself, and soon after that, he also began to snore.

Yaushu hit the ground several times with his foot. When he was sure the old man was sleeping, he slid silently out of bed and crept up to the fire. Then he reached out his tail, picked up a burning ember, and slowly backed away into the night.

He had gone quite a distance when a gale of wind swooped down upon him. The trees bent under its force; stones rolled along the ground. Yaushu ran as hard as he could, but the wind caught up to him and suddenly the Lord of Fire stood before him, trembling with rage.

"Grandson, what have you done? I warned you not to touch anything, and yet you chose to steal from your grandfather. Now it's too late, and you must die."

The Lord of Fire picked up Yaushu in his powerful hands and tried to wrest the ember from his grip. Even though the hot coals burned his tail, Yaushu did not let it go. The burning brand was like part of his body itself. The Lord of Fire stomped on him, crushed his bones, carried him up into the air and shook him, and finally threw him back down on the earth. Then, certain he had killed him, the old man returned to his cave to take care of the fire.

Yaushu rolled down the mountainside, covered in blood, throwing off sparks like a ball of fire. That was the shape he was in when he got back to the Tabaosimoa, who were still praying. More dead than alive, he unrolled his charred tail and let the embers fall to the ground. The Great Ones picked them up and lit their hearth fires.

People all around called the opossum "Yaushu the Brave," in recognition of having brought fire to humankind from the east. To this day, the fur has never grown back on his tail, and he still walks laboriously ever since that time when Grandfather Fire, with his terrible power, broke all his bones.

DEVIL'S GORGE

BY **ANA MARÍA GÜIRALDES**

An Indian legend of southern Chile

LINCARAYÉN, the chief's daughter, was the most beautiful girl in the tribe. Not only was her face lovely; everyone said that she was as graceful and pure as a quilineja flower.

That was why Quiltrapiche loved her. He watched her movements from afar, and his eyes smiled when she passed by looking for flowers to adorn her long black hair.

Nevertheless, Quiltrapiche knew that the young woman was unhappy. In fact, no one in the tribe was happy. All sense of peace and well-being had vanished completely the day the evil spirit known as Pillán had loosed his demons upon the village. How could they work the land if this destructive god sent fire raining down from the volcanoes to ruin their fields? Yet how could they risk disobeying him when he would punish them by poisoning their water with potions that deformed people's faces and made them shout in voices more harsh and croaking than the harshest of thunderbolts?

For a long time now, they had all been so frightened that they wandered about without daring to look up at the summits of the volcanoes, for fear of incurring some terrible disaster.

At night their terror grew. Enormous tongues of flame burst from the mouths of the Calbuco and Osorno volcanoes, lighting up the night sky and transforming it into a fiery hell. To those who worked in the fields, it was a warning of what might happen some day.

One afternoon the band gathered together to pray for the fertility of the soil. The voices of men, women and children were raised in supplication. All nature bowed to their yearning and accompanied their pleas, from the songs of birds and the sound of waterfalls and wind to the river waters that rippled with their prayers.

Suddenly, the wind stopped blowing and the dust remained suspended in the air. Birds broke off in the middle of their flight. The waters became calm, and the arrogant smoke of the volcanoes plunged back into the depths of the earth. So great was the silence that the only sound the people heard was that of their own rapid heartbeats as they waited to see what would happen.

Then, out of nowhere, an old man appeared. No one had ever seen him before. He walked toward them, raising his hand in greeting. When he spoke, his voice was so soft that it seemed to rise not from the throat of a man, but of a spirit.

"Pillán, the demon who is making you suffer, lives in the depths of the great volcano," he said. "Whenever you work the land, his rage is transformed into fire that slithers down the slopes of the mountain and burns up the fields you have sown. But there is a way to overcome him."

A clamor of entreaty arose from the people standing around the stranger. When they had calmed down, the old man continued.

"You must throw a branch of a cinnamon tree directly into the mouth of the volcano."

"How can we even get close to it?" protested the people. "The demon will burn us up with his flames! The land itself is afire on the slopes of that mountain. Boiling water shoots up out of the soil!"

The old man waited until they fell silent again.

"There is only one way you can reach the volcano's crater. It is by sacrificing the purest and most beautiful girl of the tribe. You must remove her heart and leave it along with the cinnamon branch on the summit of Mount Pichi Juan."

His voice became even softer. Everyone drew near so they could hear.

"When you have done this, a huge bird will appear. It will circle the mountain and then alight and devour the heart. Then it will take the cinnamon branch and fly off to Osorno Volcano, where it will drop the branch into the pit of fire. This will cause an enormous snowfall that will freeze the angry demon."

The tribe listened in suspense.

The old man's voice now took on a tone of command as he raised his finger in warning.

"But if some day the tribe should ever become lazy and slothful, the evil spirit Pillán will return, and the sacrifice will have been in vain!"

As soon as the man had pronounced these words, he disappeared as mysteriously as he had come. Then the wind scattered the dust suspended in the air. Flocks of birds flew by overhead, and whitecaps appeared on the waters of the lake.

Quiltrapiche turned to the chief, who was trembling with fear. Even the children could guess who would be chosen for the sacrifice.

"My daughter, my sweet Lincarayén," sobbed the chief.

Quiltrapiche looked at the volcano.

But the girl went up to the chief and took his hand, smiling.

"Don't worry, Father," she said softly. "I will die happy, knowing that my death will have put an end to this horror. All I ask is that you do not use spears or knives, that it be flowers and their fragrance that close my eyes forever, and that it be Quiltrapiche who then removes my heart."

The next morning, when dawn came with its avalanche of light and sound, the sacrificial procession slowly wound its way down into the depths of a deep chasm known as Devil's Gorge. Quiltrapiche was already waiting for them next to a bed of flowers that he himself had prepared. Lincarayén could see him from the edge of the gorge, and she advanced down the slope followed by the women of the tribe, who wept silently.

When they reached the bottom of the canyon, the women helped Lincarayén stretch out on the bed of flowers. One of them arranged her tunic; another spread out her long black hair over the pillow of petals. The sounds of the countryside and the voices of the people fell silent as the girl and Quiltrapiche looked lovingly into each other's eyes.

The whole tribe now sat around them and waited.

At mid-morning they saw Lincarayén's cheeks become pale.

When the sun was beyond its zenith in the sky, her eyelids closed.

A reddish color spread over the countryside, and the girl's breast barely rose and fell as she breathed in the perfume of the flowers.

The silhouettes of the trees were fading into the evening shadows when the girl finally breathed her last.

Qualtrapiche stepped forward. His hand trembled as he carried out his task. Holding Lincarayén's heart in the palms of his hands, he stepped over to the chief and handed it to him. Then he returned to the girl's prone body and, without a word, plunged his spear into his chest.

The tribe cried out in horror. But the chief, his voice breaking with sorrow, ordered a lad to cut a branch from a cinnamon tree and run with it and the girl's heart to the top of Mount Pichi Juan.

When the youth had done so and was descending the slopes of the mountain, a huge condor appeared in the sky with its wings outstretched. The bird hovered soundlessly over the mountaintop and then descended to the heart that lay bleeding atop a large rock. It ate the heart and then picked up the branch and flew off toward Osorno Volcano, which roared in the distance as flames shot up from its crater. The condor made three spiraling passes over the volcano and then dropped the branch directly into the crater.

"Look!" cried a woman, pointing up to the sky.

Black clouds began to swirl overhead. An intense cold suddenly fell over the earth, and tiny white feathers of snow began to fall.

Everything came true exactly as the old man had foretold. Deep snow gradually covered the mountain and finally blocked up the fiery crater of the volcano, and the evil spirit Pillán, after writhing with rage, fell silent forever.

The people of the tribe thought they would never again in their lives witness such an event. Yet when they returned to the place of Lincarayén's sacrifice, they were astonished by still another miracle. The flowers from the bed of blossoms had put out roots, and their stems had twined together to form the walls of an immense castle. And the people were overcome with joy to see Lincarayén and Quiltrapiche walking hand in hand among the petaled halls, united in the afterlife.

Today, the chasm known as Devil's Gorge is located near the town of Puerto Varas. Many people continue to climb down the winding path along its walls to see the incredibly lush vegetation that covers the bottom of the canyon. But only those who are as graceful and pure as the quilineja blossom are able to find the castle of flowers.

PART II

THE ENCHANTRESS OF CÓRDOBA

BY **FRANCISCO SERRANO**

A tale from colonial Mexico

TWO HUNDRED years ago there lived a beautiful black woman in the city of Córdoba, in what is now the state of Veracruz. She remained lovely and young and never seemed to grow old, no matter how many years went by.

This beautiful woman was known as Mulata. She was famous for her ability to help out people in difficulty, whether they were girls without boyfriends, workers without jobs, doctors without patients, lawyers without clients, or generals without armies. All of them would turn to Mulata for help and leave her house happy and satisfied after consulting with her.

The men who came to her for advice were captivated by her beauty and would vie with one another for her favor. But Mulata would give herself to no one and spurned all their attentions.

People whispered stories about Mulata's powers and said she was a witch and an enchantress.

Some said they had seen her flying over the rooftops, her dark eyes gleaming with a satanic light and her sensuous mouth open in a wild smile that revealed her bright red lips and strong white teeth.

Others swore that Mulata had made a pact with the devil and was often his guest. They said that those who went by her house at midnight would see a sinister light pouring out from the cracks under the windows and doors— an infernal light, as if a powerful fire were raging through the rooms inside.

Mulata's fame was enormous. She was known throughout the area, and stories were told about her even in other parts of Mexico:

> *Long ago, years ago,*
> *she lived in this part of town*
> *on a quiet little square.*

In our neighborhood? It can't be!
No one ever saw her
in a patio or doorway,
on the street or in church,
or at the market, either.
So she's not from this part of town;
she just suddenly turned up here!
In Córdoba, just when
did she unexpectedly appear?

Then one day she was arrested in Córdoba and taken to the frightful Court of the Inquisition in Mexico City, where she was tried for witchcraft and sorcery.

The morning of the day she was to be executed, the jailer entered her cell and was surprised to find that Mulata had drawn the hull of a ship with charcoal on one of the walls.

"Good morning, jailer," she said, turning to him. "Could you tell me what finishing touches my ship might need?"

"Unlucky woman!" answered the jailer. "If you repent your crimes, you won't have to die."

"Come on, just tell me. What does my ship still need?" insisted Mulata.

"How should I know? It...it needs a mast."

"If that's what it needs, then that's what it shall have," answered Mulata enigmatically.

The jailer, unable to understand what was she was up to, swung the door closed and went on about his rounds, shaking his head in confusion.

At noon, the same warder returned to Mulata's cell and looked in wonder at the ship she had drawn on the wall.

"Jailer, what does my ship need now?" asked Mulata.

"Wretched woman," answered the bewildered man. "If you really wish to save your soul from the flames of hell, you can still escape the Inquisition's sentence. What is it you want now? Your ship needs some sails."

"If that's what it needs, then that's what it shall have," answered Mulata.

At sunset, the hour that had been set for Mulata's execution, the jailer returned to her cell a third and final time.

"What does my ship need now?" asked Mulata with a smile.

"Unfortunate woman," answered the warder. "Put your soul in the hands of Our Lord God and repent your sins. All your ship needs now is just to sail away. It's perfect!"

"Well, then, if your grace so wishes and that's what he insists on, then sail away it shall, and far away at that!"

"What? How will it do so?"

"Like this," said Mulata, and quick a wink she jumped into the ship, which moved slowly at first and then picked up speed as its sails billowed in the wind. It traversed the room with its beautiful passenger and disappeared through the wall in a corner of the cell.

The jailer was dumbfounded. He stood motionless, his eyes protruding from their sockets, his hair on end, and his mouth hanging open in amazement.

No one ever again heard from Mulata. They say she went to live with the devil and that whoever believes in stories of witchcraft should try drawing ships upon the walls.

THE BLACK SHIP

BY **PABLO ANTONIO CUADRA**

A folktale from the island of Zapatera, in Lake Nicaragua

THEY say that long ago a ship crossing Lake Nicaragua from Granada to San Carlos was rounding the tip of Redonda Island when the crew suddenly saw someone on the shore signaling them with a bedsheet.

When they landed on the island, all they heard were cries of pain. Every member of the two large families that lived there, from the grandparents to the babies, was dying from food poisoning. They had all eaten the meat of a cow that had been bitten by a venomous snake.

"Take us to Granada!" they pleaded.

"Who will pay for the trip?" asked the captain.

"We don't have a penny," said those who had been poisoned. "But we'll pay you with firewood, bananas, anything!"

"Really?" said the sailors. "Who'll cut the firewood? Who'll pick the bananas?"

"I've got a load of hogs on board for Los Chiles, and if I wait too long, they'll suffocate," said the captain.

"But we're *people*," answered the dying families.

"So are we," said the crew members. "And this is how we make a living."

"For God's sake!" cried the oldest man on the island. "Can't you see that if you leave us we'll all die?"

"We've got commitments to keep," said the captain. And he and his crew returned to the boat. Even the people writhing on the ground made them feel no pity.

The sailors just left them there. But as they were going, an aged grandmother sat up in her cot and, in the strongest voice she could muster, cast a curse upon them.

"May those who have closed their hearts find the lake has closed around them!"

The ship left. Later that night it was driven offshore near San Carlos and then lost sight of land. No one aboard ever again saw the coast, or the hills, or the stars.

It is said that, for centuries now, the captain and crew have sailed endlessly back and forth, lost in the middle of the lake. The ship has turned black; its sails have rotted away and its rigging has snapped. Many people around the lake have seen it. When they are out in their boats and the waves are high, they come upon a black ship with a bearded, ragged crew that shouts, "Which way to San Jorge? Which way to Granada?"

But the wind blows them back into the middle of the lake and out of sight of land once more. They are accursed.

THE TEARS OF SOMBRERO GRANDE

BY **LUIS ALFREDO ARANGO**

A Guatemalan folktale

CELINA was a very beautiful girl. The people along Carrocero Lane, in the Belén neighborhood, saw her every day and never ceased to marvel at how lovely she was. And the older she grew, the more comely Celina became.

"What beautiful eyes!"

"Yes, and how big they are!"

"And what beautiful hair she has!"

"So long and wavy!"

"She looks like Our Lady of Socorro in the cathedral!"

It was true. Celina did look like the small statue of Our Lady of Socorro, dark-skinned and graceful. Even her name was unusual, as if fallen from the sky or taken from a story about a far-off land.

The fame of Celina's beauty began to spread all over the city. Apart from being lovely to look at, she was also a hard worker. She helped her mother make corn tortillas and take them around to sell at rich people's houses.

Seeing her running along the streets on her way to sell the tortillas was the delight of young and old men alike. They were all impressed by her.

One evening around six o'clock, at the corner of Belén Street and Carrocero Lane, four mules were found tethered to a lamppost. The mules were laden with bags of charcoal.

"Those mules look like they belong to Sombrero Grande," said one woman. She was referring to stories about a tiny man with an enormous sombrero who was said to seduce young women with his songs. He played a guitar made of mother-of-pearl and always traveled with four mules loaded with charcoal.

"For Lord's sake, don't mention his name!" said another woman as she passed by.

That night Celina felt very tired after working all day. She was just beginning

45

to drift off to sleep when she heard someone singing an exquisitely beautiful song and accompanying himself on the guitar.

"Mother! Listen to that music!" she said.

"What music? You're just getting sleepy, that's all," answered her mother.

"No, I'm not. Listen to how wonderful it is!"

But her mother never heard it.

"You'd better go to bed now, dear."

Celina couldn't sleep a wink as she listened to those enchanting songs. And now she could clearly hear the singer's melodious voice:

You're a white dove,
like the flower of the lemon tree,
and if you don't say you're mine,
I'll die of love.

By eleven that night, the lane was quiet and the four mules with the load of charcoal had disappeared into the darkness.

Night after night the same thing occurred. Most people only noticed four mules loaded with charcoal and tied to a lamppost. Celina, however, was thrilled by the songs she heard.

One night, without her mother knowing, Celina went outside to peer into the darkness and see if she could find out who was singing such sweet, melancholy songs.

She almost died of fright. It was Sombrero Grande himself! There he was, a tiny little man with a gigantic sombrero, patent-leather shoes and silver spurs. Yet as he danced and sang, playing his minuscule mother-of-pearl guitar, the girl felt herself falling in love with him:

The stars in the sky
walk two by two;
just like my eyes
when I walk behind you.

Celina couldn't sleep for the rest of the night. She wasn't able to stop thinking about Sombrero Grande. All the next day she kept remembering the words to his songs. She found that she both wanted and didn't want him to come that night. She wanted and yet didn't want to see him again. That week Celina stopped eating and stopped smiling.

"What's the matter, dear?" her mother asked. "Is something wrong? Are you sick?" But Celina didn't answer.

"She must have fallen in love with Sombrero Grande," people whispered. Her mother was becoming desperate and decided to follow the advice of her neighbors. She took the girl from the house and locked her in a church on the other side of town, where spirits would not be able to enter.

The following night Sombrero Grande arrived in Carrocero Lane, but there wasn't a trace of Celina. He became furious and began to search for her all over the city, but he couldn't find her anywhere. At dawn he departed, soundlessly, with his train of mules.

Celina's mother and neighbors were all very happy, because they had managed to free her from Sombrero Grande's spell. Celina, however, was still locked up in the church. She quickly she fell ill from her unbearable sadness and was found dead a few days later.

Everyone sat up all night with the body of the dead girl in her home. Suddenly they heard a heart-rending lament that made their blood run cold. It was Sombrero Grande with his string of mules! He stopped at the lamppost on the corner and began to weep as he sang:

> *Heart of sacred wood,*
> *branch of flowering lemon-tree,*
> *why have you left the one you love*
> *forgotten in oblivion?*
> *Aaaaaaayyy! Aaayyy!*
> *Tomorrow when you come*
> *I will go out to the road*
> *and fill your handkerchief*
> *with tears and sighs!*

No one ever knew what time it was when Sombrero Grande left. He went off slowly, weeping sorrowfully, until he vanished into the darkness of the night. In the morning, as the mourners were leaving the dead girl's house, they suddenly stopped in amazement.

There on the cobblestones of the street was a trail of crystal tears as big as raindrops, glistening in the sunlight.

ANTONIO AND THE THIEF

BY **SAUL SCHKOLNIK**

A folktale from Chile

A BOY named Antonio was playing in the hallway of his house.

His mother came and told him, "Listen, Toño, go down to the village and buy some flour and butter, because I've run out." She gave him a handful of coins. "And be careful not to lose the money!"

Antonio put the coins way down in the bottom of his pocket, picked up his poncho and hat, and headed for the town of Toconce, which lay just on the other side of the mountain. He put his hand in his pocket and held onto the coins as he walked.

He was strolling along, whistling happily, when he happened to glance over his shoulder. He noticed that a man was following him. This looked like trouble to Antonio, so as soon as he had gone around the next curve in the road, he took off his hat and put it on the ground. Then he put a large rock under it and pretended he was tying the hat down tightly around something inside.

The man who was following him—and it *was* a thief—came around the bend and stopped next to Antonio.

"Hey, what's that you've got in your hat?" the man asked.

"It's a hen. I've had to tie her up, because she's so smart that if I let her out—bam!—she'll fly right off. Could you hold her down for me for a few minutes? I want to go and get a cage."

Hmm, thought the bandit. When this dumb kid is gone, I'll have his hen without even going to the trouble of robbing him. He must not have anything else worth much. And squatting down, he put his hands firmly over the hat. Antonio quickly walked off.

The thief waited until the boy was out of sight. Then he gingerly raised one side of the hat, slipped his hand underneath and grabbed the rock. "Ouch!" he cried. There wasn't any hen.

49

Now he was mad. "That kid tricked me," he exclaimed, "He's going to pay for this when I get hold of him." He put the hat on his head and took off down the road after Antonio.

A short while later, Antonio looked over his shoulder and saw that the same man was catching up to him again. He climbed up the hillside just above the road where a boulder stuck out of the ground. He took off his poncho and spread it out on top of the rock. Then he put his shoulder to it, as if he were trying with all his might to hold it back.

The robber came up and stopped below where the boy was standing.

"Hey, what are you doing with that rock?" he asked.

"Watch out!" warned Antonio. "This rock is going to fall, and if it does it will crush us both and roll right down onto the town of Toconce. Could you hold it back for awhile? I'm going to get some stakes."

The thief became frightened and put his shoulder against Antonio's poncho and began pushing the rock back with all his might. He held that position for quite a while, but the boy seemed to be taking an awfully long time coming back.

Wait a minute! thought the thief. Of course the lad would take a while. He would have to run all the way down to the town and back. "Ouf! I'm getting tired," he said to himself. "I think I'll just let this rock go. I'm so worn out from holding it back that I don't care if it crushes me or the town." He let go of the rock and it didn't move a bit.

"That kid tricked me again," he cried, getting madder and madder. "This time when I catch up to him, I'll steal everything he has and give him a beating, too." He took off running after the boy.

Antonio was now just coming into town. He could see the houses with their stone walls and thatched roofs scattered across the green valley and surrounded by arid mountains. As he got closer, there were more and more plants and locust trees alongside the road. He looked over his shoulder again and saw the thief running after him. He quickly stepped up to a locust tree and began plaiting a rope.

The bandit came up to where Antonio was standing.

"Hey, what are you doing with that rope?" he asked.

"I'm weaving it together so it will be stronger," answered Antonio. "The earth is about to turn upside down and we're all going to fall off except for

51

these locust trees. That's why I'm going to tie myself nice and tight to this tree right here."

"Really?" said the thief, feeling quite uneasy. And he thought to himself, If the earth does turn upside-down, it won't be me who falls off. He turned back to Antonio.

"Listen, tie me to the tree first. Then you can tie yourself afterward if you want," he told the boy.

Antonio made it look as if he was thinking this over.

"All right!" he said finally. "I'll tie you up first. Put your arms around the tree and hold on tight."

The thief did as Antonio told him and the boy bound him tightly to the tree.

"Don't pull the rope so taut," complained the thief, but Antonio kept on making it tighter. When he had finished tying up the thief, he went down to the village, bought the flour and butter, and started home again. He came back to the place where the thief was still tied to the tree.

"Hey!" said the robber. "When did you say the earth was going to turn upside-down?"

"Any time now! Any minute!" the boy replied. "But until it does, I think I'll take back my hat and poncho, because it's starting to get cold." He took his hat off the bandit's head and picked up his poncho. Then he put them on and continued on his way back home, whistling happily.

PEDRO RIMALES, THE HEALER

BY **RAFAEL RIVERO ORAMAS**

A folktale from Venezuela

ONE DAY Pedro Rimales arrived in a faraway country, all tired out and without a penny. He decided to try to pass for a healer so he could earn a few *reales* and not starve to death.

"Who knows?" he said to himself. "Maybe I'll even become rich and powerful."

He started up a rumor that he was a man of great learning who knew all the illnesses that had ever been or ever would be and that he could cure them with his mysterious medicines.

But nobody came to see him, even to cure a cold.

Then Pedro found out that the king of this far-off land was obsessed with the idea that he himself was an expert doctor. The king believed that every sick person in his domain should take his prescriptions, whether they wanted to or not.

"So much the better," said Pedro. "If I'm able to cure some sick person that the king is unable to heal, I may even get to be king myself."

And then one morning it so happened that a certain man in that faraway land woke up with an overpowering feeling of laziness and without the slightest inclination to go to work.

"I'm dying," he cried, and fell to the ground as if he really were dead.

Whenever anybody came near him, the man held his breath and made his body stiff.

"He's dead," everyone said.

Pedro Rimales began to watch him. When no one was around, the dead man's shirtfront would rise and fall with his breathing—up and down, up and down.

"Why don't you ask the king to cure him?" suggested Pedro.

"Why would we do that? Are you crazy? Can't you see this man is dead?"

Pedro smiled mysteriously and said, "Death is a sickness that can be cured like any other. Of course, you have to know how."

Everybody was stunned. Was there really someone able to cure death itself?

"All right, then," one of them said. "Heal this man here who has just died."

"I would," said Pedro, "but the king might not like it. He might even have me put to death."

"If you can cure him, so can the king," they replied.

And they went to get the king.

The king arrived in a coach loaded with jars of ointments and boxes full of powders and magic herbs. He had the dead man plied with smelling salts and anointed with pomades. He even tried to get the dead man to drink a special potion. But the patient had now become so lazy that he had grown tired of playing dead and had fallen into a deep sleep. None of the king's concoctions could awaken him.

The king furiously called for Pedro Rimales.

"Now you try," the king told him. "But if you can't get this dead man to stand up, I'll see that you get a thrashing. After that, you won't want to go around passing yourself off as a healer anymore."

Pedro put leaves from different plants into a *tapara* gourd and mixed them with water from the river. Then he lit a cigar and blew smoke into the gourd three times. He stepped up to the dead man and poured the medicine into his mouth. At the same time, without anyone seeing, he put out the cigar on the man's behind. When the dead man felt the terrible pain of the burning cigar, he let out a tremendous yell and leaped to his feet in one jump.

Nobody could believe their eyes. They all proclaimed Pedro Rimales king and presented him with the royal robe and crown.

Pedro Rimales reigned for several years in that distant land, until one day he grew tired of greeting ambassadors and dancing waltzes and decided to leave. He took off the robe and crown and set off again to see the world.

THE HORSE OF SEVEN COLORS

BY **HÉCTOR FELIPE CRUZ CORZO**

A folktale from Guatemala

DON ISIDRO'S farm was at the foot of the mountain. It was a large, prosperous, clean farm. His vegetables were the finest in the area, and the neighboring farmers visited him regularly to see if they could learn his secrets.

One night, Don Isidro and his three sons heard a drove of horses cavorting about in his vegetable patch. They lit their lamps, shouldered their hunting rifles and went outside to see what was going on. What a shock they had when they found the plot filled with horses of all different colors! They fired their guns at them but, since they were enchanted horses, the bullets turned into mist. At the sound of the shots, the horses ran from the garden, which they had damaged a great deal, and galloped off without a trace, as if they had flown away through the air.

At dawn, Don Isidro and his sons returned to the vegetable plot and were very sad to find so many plants crushed and bruised. They seeded it again and Don Isidro told his oldest son, who was named Juan, to keep watch over the field at night. Juan tried to do as he was told, but toward the middle of the night he nodded off into a deep sleep. The next morning the newly seeded vegetable garden was all torn up again.

When Don Isidro found out what had happened, he scolded his son severely.

"You're completely useless, a real good-for-nothing!" he told him.

"It wasn't my fault, Father. I smelled a sweet scent of night-blooming flowers and was suddenly overcome by a strange, deep sleep," his son answered.

"Well, tonight I want *you* to watch the field," the father said to his second son, who was named Carlos.

"All right, Father," Carlos answered.

But, just as had happened the night before, a strange aroma, something like that of night jasmine, spread out over the farmland, and Carlos fell asleep. The horses returned and trampled all the vegetables.

When he saw his newly seeded field devastated once again, Don Isidro went into an uncontrollable rage.

"You're a slacker, too!" he upbraided his second son.

"It wasn't my fault, Father," said Carlos. "While I was keeping watch, a fresh, delicate smell began to waft through the air, and then I fell into a fathomless sleep, completely against my will."

"Now, listen, tonight I want *you* to keep watch," Don Isidro said to José, the youngest of his three sons.

"All right, Father," replied José.

José, who was very clever, devised a plan to keep from falling asleep. He would catch the horses unawares and maybe even capture one of them. He hung a hammock between two orange trees, filled it with stinging nettles, and lay down. Just as he began to smell the same sweet, penetrating scent and was starting to doze off, the fiery pain from rubbing against the nettles became so intense that he felt wide awake again.

He was still scratching from the nettles when the herd of multi-colored horses entered the vegetable plot. José was amazed by how wonderful they were. But, quick as ever, he jumped up, grabbed a rope, and before you could say "Bless you!" had already lassoed the most beautiful horse of all. It looked as if it had been painted with a rainbow.

The horse of seven colors whinnied and struggled to get away but couldn't, because José had tied a small cross made of *ocote* pine onto the rope. Gradually it calmed down until it was as tame as a Castillian dove. The other horses saw that their leader had been captured and fled in fright.

When the horse of seven colors saw that he couldn't get free, he proposed a deal to José.

"Let me go," he said, "and I'll give you whatever you ask."

"I can't," the boy replied. "You're too sly for that, and besides, you'll have to answer to my father for all the mischief you've caused."

"Let me go, and I'll make the vegetable patch even better than it was before we came," said the horse. "What's more, I'll promise to help you out of whatever trouble you may someday have."

"Before I accept, fix up the garden," said José.

"All right. Look carefully and listen: *White rocks, smooth rocks, eyes of stone curlew, the finest of all vegetables will arise now for you.*"

And there immediately sprouted up the most beautiful produce that José had ever seen. When he had overcome his astonishment, the boy turned again to the horse.

"I can see you really do have magic powers," he said. "I'll let you go, because a horse as beautiful as you should never be a prisoner. But promise me you'll never again trample my father's vegetables."

"I promise."

José set the horse free, and it disappeared like a colored paper balloon carried off by the wind.

At five o'clock that morning, Don Isidro and his two other sons came down to see the vegetables and were amazed to find them more beautiful than ever.

"You see," Don Isidro told his sons, "my youngest boy is a true hero!" And he ran over and embraced José.

In the days that followed, the two other sons became jealous of José's success, and decided to run away from the farm. One night they left and never came back. Don Isidro was so heartbroken that he fell ill, and José had to go out in search of his brothers. When he finally found them, they grabbed him by the hands and feet and threw him into a deep well.

He would certainly have drowned, but he remembered the horse of seven colors and called out to him. The horse instantly appeared and saved him.

José ran off again after his brothers, and when he caught up to them they looked at each other in disbelief, for they couldn't understand how he had managed to get out of the well.

"Brothers, Father has fallen ill because he misses you so much," José told them.

"Who cares?" they answered. "He still has his favorite little boy to take care of things." And they went off into the mountains. José followed them, pleading with them to come home.

As they passed a spring, they saw a royal decree nailed to the trunk of a trumpetwood tree:

WHOSOEVER WINS THE PRINCESS'S GOLD RING IN TOMORROW'S
HORSE RACE SHALL RECEIVE HER HAND IN MARRIAGE!

The competition that was to be held was not a usual horse race. A long rope was to be hung between two buildings, and the princess's ring would be suspended from a thread attached to it. Each rider would ride out separately and gallop forward and try to spear the princess's ring on a long silver needle. The princess's finger was very slender, and many great horsemen had tried in the past to win her ring without success.

The two older brothers decided to enter the race. They made José their servant and had him wash and groom their horses.

The next day, Juan and Carlos mounted their horses and told José, "When we come back, we want pork chops and fried potatoes for lunch!"

"Can't I go and watch the race, too?" asked José.

"No!" they answered and rode off, laughing loudly.

José was so sad that he didn't feel like doing anything. Then he suddenly remembered his friend, the horse of seven colors. He called him, and the horse instantly appeared.

"What can I do for you?" the horse asked.

"I want to ride you in the race and win the golden ring so I can marry the princess," José replied.

"It'll be a pleasure," said the horse, and they set off for the palace.

All the other horses had already run, without a single rider being able to pass the silver needle through the princess's golden ring. Suddenly, the announcer called out, "Bring on the final contestant!"

The spectators fell silent as the horse of seven colors trotted past with silver-plated hooves, a velvet-covered saddle, and a rider dressed in silk and gold. Horse and rider won the ring with ease, leaving a wonderful aroma in the air as they flashed by.

"That man shall be my son-in-law!" cried the king from the palace balcony, and the princess was seen to blush.

Minutes later, José rode up to the palace with the golden ring, and the following day the marriage ceremony took place in the great chapel of the palace. José called for his brothers to appear before him; he forgave them and asked them to go back and get their father so they could all live at the royal palace. And the horse of seven colors disappeared, as if by magic.

BLANCA AND THE WILD MAN

BY **VERÓNICA URIBE** AND **CARMEN DIANA DEARDEN**

A folktale from Venezuela

BLANCA had a head of curly hair and eyes that were somewhere between green and yellow. She was pretty, but strange. She walked about absent-mindedly and almost never spoke, not even on the day her grandmother took her and the other children to swim in the Coral Snake swimming hole, deep in the forest.

The boys walked ahead, whittling tree branches into spears to kill the coral snakes that were always found near the swimming hole. The girls followed, laughing and joking. Last of all came Blanca, listening to the noises of the forest: its squeaks, moans and whispering leaves. From time to time she would stop and turn around, because she had the feeling someone was following her, that there were eyes or a voice or a shadow hidden in the leaves that shimmered in the morning sun.

"Come on, Blanca," called her grandmother. "Hurry up!"

But Blanca was the last one to arrive at the swimming place, the last to take off her clothes, and the last to jump into the dark, murmuring water. Even there, in the middle of the natural pool, it seemed as if someone was watching her or calling her from the treetops beyond the shore.

"You have to watch out for the Wild Man who lives in the woods and casts spells on beautiful young women," the village girls used to say.

And Blanca, curled up on a stone that was warm with sunlight, her hair filled with shining droplets, saw the eyes of a jaguar and the feet of a deer moving silently through the underbrush.

Suddenly a warm wind came up, and something became entangled in her hair. She jumped up in alarm, and a bright orange blossom from a *bucare* tree fell from her hair. She looked up. The wind was moving through the branches in the very top of the tree. That was all.

61

Blanca never went back to the swimming hole and never even entered the forest again.

"Hey, Blanca, let's go swimming," the other girls would say.

"Go ahead, child," her grandmother would insist. But Blanca would softly shake her head and spend the day alone in the silent house.

"She's afraid of the Wild Man," the other girls laughed.

"No, I'm not. I'm not afraid of him," Blanca said one day, but nobody heard her.

The days went by.

In the afternoon, Blanca would come out onto the porch. She would sit in her grandmother's rocking chair and look far off into the distance, beyond the river, where the thick jungle began. The motion of the rocking chair and the cool air on her face would make her remember once again the play of light and shadow in the forest, and once again she would hear the squeaks and moans and whisperings. And if she closed her eyes tight and breathed very softly, it also seemed as if someone very strong were lifting her up, up above the trunks and highest branches of the trees, until she could see the river and the village down below, small and far away.

"What's wrong with that girl? She always seems so distant," said her grandmother one afternoon, as she watched Blanca rocking on the chair and softly smiling.

"It's nothing," answered Blanca's mother. "What could ever come of dreaming like that? It's just something girls her age go through."

"Maybe she's been bewitched by the Wild Man," replied the grandmother. "They say he casts spells on girls just like a boa constrictor. And when he's turned their minds, he throws them over his hairy shoulder and takes them back to the jungle."

"Those are just stories. No one's ever seen the Wild Man."

"Well, somebody must have seen him, because they say he's as hairy as a bear, half monkey and half man, with the eyes of a jaguar and the feet of a deer."

Then, one afternoon, just past sunset on the day after her fifteenth birthday, Blanca disappeared. No one ever knew what happened. There wasn't any sound, or voices, or cries. People said that the girl's grandmother had been right. The Wild Man came quietly up on footsteps of mist, threw Blanca over his back and walked across the waters of the river. Then he took her to live in the house high in the treetops that he had built just for her. And there he brings her fruit and berries and adorns her hair with flowers and endlessly licks the soles of her feet.

And no one ever knew whether Blanca never returned because she was so weak and afraid or because she just didn't want to come down from the Wild Man's enchanted treehouse.